Dear Reader,

Thank you for checking out Little Rhino! I'm so excited about this book series. I know the first question you have is, are these stories real? Krystle and I wanted to tell a fun story about a boy who loves baseball. Not everything in these books happened to me but a lot of it is based on my life!

I'll never forget my first Little League baseball team, the Mustangs. That was the first time my friends and I had our last names and numbers on our jerseys. It made me feel like a real pro baseball player. It was our own "little big league" with bat bags, uniforms, and jackets, just like the professional players had on TV.

I wasn't allowed to go to baseball practice until my homework was done so it was the first thing I did when I got home from school. Homework before practice. Good grades before baseball games. Those were the rules growing up.

Every kid on the team had different talents they brought to the baseball field, but it was most important to have fun playing the game. Enjoy the time you spend with your teammates, work together, and always try your best!

Krystle Howard

LITTLE
Rhino

LITTLE

Rhino

by RYAN HOWARD
and KRYSTLE HOWARD

BOOK ONE
MY NEW TEAM

SCHOLASTIC INC.

To those who dream big. Dreams can come true.

—R.H. & K.H.

ISBN 978-0-545-67490-4

12 11 10 9 8 7 6 5 4 3   15 16 17 18 19 20/0

Printed in the U.S.A.   40

First printing, February 2015
Book design by Christopher Stengel

· CHAPTER 1 ·
Three Seconds

Little Rhino stepped up to home plate. He gripped the bat tight. The breeze in the treetops sounded like the crowd at a Major League Baseball game. He imagined that the bases were loaded.

Hit this one out of the park, he told himself.

Rhino glared at the pitcher. Here came the ball!

With a hard, steady swing, Rhino connected. The smack of the bat against the ball sent a thrill through his body.

"Nice hit!" said Grandpa James with a smile.

Rhino smiled back. He dropped the plastic bat and watched as the ball flew over the tall hedge.

He'd hit it out of the backyard! Rhino had never hit one that far before.

Grandpa pitched to Rhino every day after Rhino's homework was done. "Books first, baseball second" was the rule in their house. Rhino always raced home from third grade, had a snack, and did his work. Then he changed into shorts and an oversized jersey, grabbed his bat and glove, and met Grandpa in the yard.

"You're really hitting them now, Rhino," Grandpa said. Rhino's real name was Ryan but everyone except his teachers used his nickname. "Better get that ball before it rolls all the way to Main Street!"

Rhino laughed. He knew the ball hadn't gone that far. It was just a plastic one—not like the real MLB baseball they used for playing catch. He hit with a plastic one because a real one might break a window. That would be bad.

Rhino trotted out of the yard. He stopped cold when he saw Dylan on the other side of the street.

Dylan was tall and thin and always looked mean. He was holding Rhino's ball.

"Looking for this?" Dylan said with a sneer. "Come and get it, wimp."

Rhino gulped. Dylan was the meanest kid in third grade. He teased everyone and often got into fights. *Dylan acts tough, but he's not,* Rhino's thinker said. Grandpa James would always point to his head and say, "Your thinker is there to think the things you can't say out loud."

Still, Dylan was bigger than Rhino. He was always sneering, his glasses sitting crooked on his face, and his stiff blond hair stood up on his head, making him look even taller.

"Come on over," Dylan said. "Come get your baby ball."

Rhino looked back. The leafy hedge blocked Grandpa's view. Rhino couldn't return to the backyard without the ball. He swallowed hard and walked across the street.

Rhino reached for the ball. Dylan held out

his hand, then pulled it away. Rhino reached again. Dylan twisted and waved the ball over his head.

"Give me the ball," Rhino said. Inside his head, his thinker added, *You big bully.*

Dylan held the ball out again. "Take it," he said.

Rhino put his hand on the ball. Dylan wouldn't let go.

"Let me have it," Rhino said. *This is why you have zero friends, Dylan,* he thought. *You're nothing but a big-mouthed bully.*

"Just take it," Dylan said. But he gripped the ball harder.

Rhino frowned and squinted his brown eyes. He pulled the ball, but Dylan just laughed. He was stronger than Rhino.

Rhino heard Grandpa's voice from the yard. "Rhino?" he said. "Is everything all right?"

Dylan looked surprised when he heard Rhino's grandfather. He yanked the ball away, then threw it

at Rhino. It hit Rhino's chest and fell to the street. Rhino scooped it up.

Dylan was walking away fast. Rhino had never seen Dylan back down from something before. He didn't look back.

Rhino stepped into the yard. Grandpa James had come closer to the hedge. He raised his bushy eyebrows but didn't say anything.

Rhino felt shaky. He didn't like uncomfortable situations. If Grandpa hadn't been there, Dylan might have started a fight. Or he might have kept the ball.

"Ready to hit some more?" Grandpa said. He gripped an imaginary bat, flexing his arm muscles, and making a powerful swing. Grandpa had always been very fit and athletic.

Rhino slowly walked back over to Grandpa. "I think I've had enough for today," he said softly.

"Really?" Grandpa asked. "You usually want to hit until it gets dark out."

Rhino shrugged. "I guess I'm tired." He felt

embarrassed because Dylan had picked on him and Rhino didn't get a chance to stand up for himself. He had let his thinker do all of his arguing, and then his grandfather showed up. Grandpa James probably heard the whole thing.

Grandpa put his hand on Rhino's shoulder. "Three seconds," he said.

Grandpa had taught Rhino the "three second rule." When you're angry or feeling bad about yourself, take three seconds to be upset. Then remember how great you are.

Rhino let his shoulders drop. He blew out his breath.

"Let's do some throwing," Grandpa said. He picked up a hardball and watched Rhino grab his glove off the lawn.

"Sounds good," Rhino said. After a few throws he felt better.

Grandpa tossed the ball high in the air. Pop flies like those were the hardest ones for Rhino to catch. The daylight was fading. Rhino set himself under the ball and watched as it reached its highest point. The ball seemed to hang in midair for a second. Then it dropped. Rhino made the catch.

"Nice one," Grandpa said.

Last month, when they'd started practicing baseball, Rhino almost never caught a pop fly. Now he grabbed them every time.

"You've made a lot of progress," Grandpa said. "Everything takes time and practice. Catching pop-ups. Hitting the ball."

Rhino nodded. Then he remembered the clash with Dylan. He stared toward the hedge and replayed the conflict. *I should have told him to get lost,* he thought.

"Everything takes time, Little Rhino," Grandpa said again. "Even dealing with a bully."

· CHAPTER 2 ·
Dinosaurs & Pizza for Lunch

Little Rhino was hungry. He glanced at the clock on the wall of the classroom. It would be lunch-time soon.

Rhino usually brought his own lunch. But Friday was pizza day. Grandpa James had given him money to buy a few slices.

"All right, class," said Mrs. Imburgia. "Time to line up."

Rhino and his friend Cooper quickly went to the front of the room.

"Ryan and Cooper, you're always first!" Mrs. Imburgia said with a laugh.

"We're always the hungriest!" said Cooper.

"And the fastest," added Rhino. They hurried to the cafeteria.

"Cheesy pizza today," said Rhino. "My most favorite thing in the entire world!"

Cooper handed a lunch tray to Rhino. Both boys could eat a lot of pizza even though Cooper was taller. They were both strong and quick. It was an even match when they played one-on-one basketball or had a race.

Rhino tilted his head back and took a deep breath of pizza aroma. "Let's eat with a new group today," he said. "Some kids from another class talk about dinosaurs at lunch. They asked me to join them."

Dinosaurs and baseball were Rhino's favorite topics but he liked learning all kinds of new facts, like how much an elephant weighs or how far the moon is from the Earth.

Rhino usually made friends easily. Cooper was shy, but he and Rhino always got along.

Cooper seemed unsure about joining the new group. "We could talk about dinosaurs by ourselves," he said.

"This will be more fun," Rhino said. "You'll see."

Rhino took a slice of pizza and a carton of milk. Then he saw Dylan getting in the line. Rhino hurried to pay. He got away from the lunch line and glanced back to make sure Dylan wasn't following him.

Rhino saw the kids in the dinosaur group waving toward him. He looked around for Cooper and saw him standing in the middle of the cafeteria.

"Cooper!" Rhino called. "Over here."

There were only two seats left at the table. Rhino set down his tray. Cooper slowly walked over and sat down in the last empty seat. Rhino looked at his friend and then at the rest of the table. The other kids were talking about T. rex.

The girl next to him nudged Rhino with her

elbow. "Hi," she said. "I'm Bella." She had a dark ponytail and a red hairband.

Rhino smiled. He was a little unsure about joining the new group, too. He felt like a family of butterflies was flying around his stomach. "I'm Ryan," he said to Bella. "But call me Rhino."

"T. rex was as long as a school bus!" said a boy with curly red hair.

"Longer than that," said a girl in a purple sweatshirt.

"No, it wasn't," said the boy. "It was forty feet long."

Rhino knew that was true. "T. rex could eat a triceratops in just a few bites," he said. Rhino took a big bite of his pizza slice. "Just like that," he added, even though his mouth was full and a string of cheese was hanging off his chin.

"They ate stegosaurs, too," said the red-haired boy.

Rhino knew that wasn't right. T. rex had lived millions of years before the stegosaurs. Rhino

started to speak, but stopped. He didn't want to have an argument on his first day with the new group. He took a sip of milk instead.

Bella nudged him again. "No stegosaurs, right?" she whispered.

Rhino shook his head gently and smiled.

Bella spoke up. "Stegosaurs didn't live at the same time as T. rex."

"They didn't?" asked the boy.

Bella shook her head. "Nope."

The boy shrugged. He started talking about how short T. rex's arms were.

After lunch, Rhino put his hand on Cooper's shoulder. "That was fun," he said. "Nice group, huh?"

Cooper nodded.

"Join in more next time," Rhino said. "You know as much about dinosaurs as any of us."

"I'll try," Cooper said.

They walked past Dylan's lunch table. "Hey, baby ball," Dylan said.

Rhino ignored him. He felt like calling Dylan "scaredy-pants" for the way he left so quickly when Grandpa James came over. But he knew that wouldn't help anything. Dylan was a bully.

"What was that about?" Cooper asked as they entered their classroom.

"Dylan was just looking for trouble," Rhino said. "He's always saying something mean."

"That's for sure," Cooper said. "I'm glad he's not in our class."

There were a few minutes until the bell for the next period. Rhino looked through his desk until he found his dinosaur book. He checked some facts about T. rex. Most of what the other kids had said was correct. Rhino knew a lot more, too.

Rhino turned to Cooper, who sat behind him. He knew that Cooper could have a lot to say about sports or music or almost anything else when they were alone. But Cooper stayed shy and quiet around most other kids.

I know how that can be, Rhino's thinker said. He could talk all day with Cooper or with Grandpa James or with his older brother, C.J. But his words didn't always come out easily, like when he had to deal with Dylan.

He'd show his dinosaur book to Cooper so he could learn some new facts. That would help Cooper to share what he knew at lunchtime. Cooper just needed some practice in talking to other kids.

Maybe Rhino needed practice, too, so he'd be ready next time Dylan tried to bully him. He wasn't afraid of Dylan, but he always seemed to be tongue-tied around him. Rhino needed his thinker to tell him what to say.

CHAPTER 3

Swing, Batter, Batter

After school, Rhino did his math homework. Then he read for thirty minutes for his reading homework. He kept thinking about hitting baseballs.

After thirty minutes, his buzzer went off. That meant he was done with his reading. Little Rhino rushed outside. Grandpa James was waiting.

"I'm going to smack every pitch into the street!" Rhino said. "Just like yesterday."

Grandpa smiled. "Let's warm up first." He tossed the ball into the air and caught it in his glove. "Get ready."

Rhino put on his glove. He felt loose and excited today. His throws had more zip on them. He caught every ball Grandpa threw, even when Grandpa made it tough by throwing them wide or high.

"All right, let's bat," Grandpa said.

Rhino tapped the plastic bat on the ground. He pulled it back toward his shoulder and waited for the pitch. He planned to hit it out of the yard. *See ya, wouldn't want to be ya.* Little Rhino sent that thought to the ball.

Rhino swung harder than ever. But instead of a solid *crack*, he heard nothing but a *swish*.

"Strike one!" came a voice from the driveway.

Rhino turned to look. His brother, C.J., was walking over with a big grin. C.J. was twelve years old and looked like a bigger version of Rhino—long legs and lean. They both looked a lot like Grandpa, too, but Grandpa's skin was darker. C.J. was left-handed, just like Rhino.

"Nice swing," C.J. said. "I felt the breeze all the way over here."

Rhino laughed. His brother was always joking like that.

"I'll take the outfield," C.J. said.

"Better go *way* back," Rhino said. "And be ready to jump."

C.J. trotted to a space in front of the hedge.

Grandpa threw another pitch.

Rhino locked his eyes on the ball. He swung as hard as before. But the bat barely nicked the ball. It went straight to the ground and rolled a few feet.

Rhino shook his head.

"Just meet the ball," Grandpa said. "It will go if you hit it solid."

Rhino was frustrated. He wanted to show C.J. how hard he could hit. He gripped the bat tighter.

He missed the next pitch completely.

"Too hard," Grandpa said. "Just make contact with the ball. The power will take care of itself."

"I'm getting bored out here!" C.J. called. He waved at Rhino and smiled.

Rhino dug in and waited. Grandpa was right. Rhino took a steady swing at the next pitch and lined it toward the hedge. C.J. grabbed it on one bounce and tossed it back.

Rhino hit the next three pitches. C.J. caught two of them on the fly. The other bounced all the way to the hedge.

I'm in the zone now, Rhino thought. *This next one is out of here!*

He put all of his might into the next swing. *Boooom!* He knocked the pitch over the hedge.

"Good-bye, Mr. Baseball!" C.J. said as he watched it go. "Nice one, Rhino!"

"See?" Grandpa said. "You've got plenty of power, Little Rhino. Just meet the ball. You see the result."

C.J. came back with the ball. Rhino wondered if Dylan had been out there again. Dylan would never mess with a guy as big as C.J.

"You put a dent in the ball!" C.J. said. "You smacked it so hard."

"Really?" Rhino asked.

C.J. laughed. "Nah. But it went clear across the street."

Rhino kept batting for a half hour. He hit two more over the hedge. Then they went inside to eat dinner.

"I have a surprise for you," Grandpa said as he poured some orange juice. "What's your favorite thing to do, Little Rhino?" Rhino and C.J. were seated around the big dinner table, passing a bowl of mac 'n' cheese around.

"Hit baseballs," Rhino said out loud. Then he thought, *And think about how I am going to be in the majors one day. Play professional baseball. Win a million World Series, be the MVP every season, and—*

"How would you like to be on a real team?" Grandpa asked.

"What?! Yes!" Rhino could picture himself in a new baseball uniform, with a team hat. He'd blast home runs and steal bases. He'd dive for line drives.

"Sign-ups for the Wildwood city league are on Saturday," Grandpa said. "There will also be a clinic to teach you young players the basics of the game."

Rhino couldn't believe it. He'd be playing baseball in a league.

"It's a great program," C.J. said. "I played in that league for four years." Now he was on the baseball team at his middle school.

"I can't wait," Rhino said. "Can we practice some more now?"

"We've done enough for today," Grandpa said. "Did you finish all of your homework?"

"Yes." But Rhino wasn't sure if he'd done enough. He had started to daydream during his thirty minutes of reading because he wanted to hit baseballs. He knew he should read the story again. "I'll read some more after dinner," he said.

"Books first," Grandpa said with a smile.

"Baseball second," Rhino added.

After dinner, Rhino read the book again. He understood it much better this time. Then he sat on his bed with his baseball glove. He held the ball in his hand. When he looked in the mirror, he imagined himself in a full baseball uniform. Tomorrow, that dream would come true.

· CHAPTER 4 ·
Practice Makes a Great Player

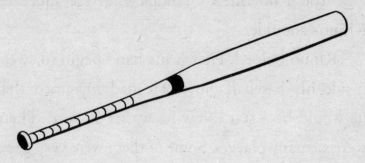

The baseball field was loaded with kids. Some were taller than him and others looked really fast. Rhino saw many boys and girls he knew, but there were some that he'd never seen before.

"This will be great," said Cooper. He'd walked to the field with Rhino and Grandpa James. "Let's get out there."

Cooper wasn't shy when it came to playing sports. He didn't have to talk much then. He let his sports skills do his talking for him. He ran onto the field and slapped hands with a couple of boys.

Rhino stood next to Grandpa and watched. *Am I ready for this?* he wondered.

"You'll do fine," Grandpa said. He squeezed Rhino's shoulder.

Rhino gulped. He felt his hand begin to sweat inside his baseball glove. He had imagined that he would be a star. Now he wasn't so sure. There were so many players. Some of them were very good athletes.

"Let's sign up," Grandpa said. He put on his glasses and steered Rhino toward a table. Several adults were helping kids fill out forms.

Rhino kept looking around as Grandpa filled out the papers. Kids were running and tossing baseballs around. They all looked confident. Rhino saw Dylan in the outfield. Dylan hadn't seen him. *He better not get in the way of my playing baseball,* Rhino's thinker said.

A man in a red jacket and a black baseball cap blew a whistle. He called for all of the players to take seats in the bleachers.

"We'll break into four groups," the man said. "Everyone will get a chance at each station. We'll show you the basics of throwing and catching, fielding a grounder, batting, and running the bases. Then you'll find out which team you're on. Next week you'll begin having practice sessions with your coach."

Cooper tapped Rhino on the arm. "Let's get in the same group," he said.

Rhino and Cooper went to the throwing and catching station first.

"I'm Coach Ray," said the man in charge of the first station. He showed them how to step toward the target when throwing the ball and to catch it securely in the web of the glove.

Rhino and Cooper already knew those basics. But not every kid did. They split into pairs and threw the ball back and forth. Coach Ray went from pair to pair to help. He was friendly but serious. "I see you're a lefty," Coach said to Rhino. "Do you bat left-handed, too?"

Rhino nodded. He felt better now. He was glad to be paired with Cooper. They were good at this.

Rhino struggled a bit at the next station. Fielding grounders wasn't so easy, and he hadn't tried that skill much at home. *I'll nail this with a little practice,* he thought. The coach at this station showed him how to crouch correctly and get behind the ball. "Take a step toward it and keep your glove wide open," said the coach.

This was fun. Rhino fielded the next three balls that came his way. He did very well at running the bases, too. Rhino was fast.

Batting was harder. Rhino didn't have much experience hitting a hardball. The bat was heavier than the one he was used to. But he hit a few grounders and popped one up. He only missed the ball a few times.

They spent about twenty minutes at each station. It was clear to Rhino that a few of the players were better than he was. Some others were just

beginners. Rhino could tell that he was better at some things than others.

"Can't wait to be in a real game," Cooper said. "I hope I get to pitch."

Rhino wasn't sure which position he'd like. Infielders had to deal with lots of ground balls. He'd done all right with that, but he was better at catching flies. *I'd probably do best in the outfield.*

The man in the red jacket blew his whistle again. "We'll break into teams now," he said. "Listen for your name. These first players will be on the Mustangs. If you hear your name, report to Coach Ray in right field."

Rhino and Cooper didn't need to wait long. They both were assigned to the Mustangs. Rhino raced to right field when he heard his name. Cooper soon followed.

Rhino recognized one other player on the team. It was Bella from the dinosaur group at school. The same family of butterflies flew back into his stomach.

"That's my dad," Bella said, pointing to Coach Ray. "He's super nice."

"That's good," Rhino said. He'd already learned a lot from Coach Ray.

Coach clapped his hands and said, "All right, Mustangs. This will be a great season."

Rhino had a big grin. He could tell that being on a team would be fun. He'd learn a lot and get to compete. Cooper and Bella would be nice teammates.

Coach looked at his clipboard. He counted the players in the group. "Someone's missing," he said. He raised his head and looked toward the infield. "Here he comes," Coach said.

Rhino turned to look. Then his heart sank. No way! He could hear that bigmouth talking from a mile away.

Dylan was trotting over to join the Mustangs!

· CHAPTER 5 ·
Bigmouthed Bully

On Monday, Rhino waited for Cooper in the cafeteria. Cooper was in the lunch line, but Rhino had brought a peanut butter and jelly sandwich from home.

"Ready for today's practice?" came a nasty voice.

Rhino turned to see Dylan staring at him.

"You won't even be able to lift the bat," Dylan said. He laughed. "It weighs a lot more than that baby one you use at home."

"I know that," Rhino said. *Bigmouth*, Rhino's thinker added. Rhino wasn't worried. He'd batted with a real wooden bat at the tryouts.

34

"You'll strike out every time," Dylan said. "I hope the coach keeps you on the bench."

"Everybody plays the same amount," Rhino said. He stood a little taller and glared at Dylan. "That's what the coach told us."

"Well, if the coach is smart, he'll forget that rule," Dylan said.

Dylan jumped when Cooper nudged him from behind. Cooper was just as big as Dylan and not afraid. "You got a problem over here?" Cooper asked Dylan.

"Just my teammate," Dylan said. He jutted his chin toward Rhino.

"He's my teammate, too," Cooper said. "I don't see that as a problem."

Dylan walked away without saying another word.

"He's annoying," Cooper said.

Rhino just shook his head. "Let's go to the dino table," he said.

"Again?" Cooper replied.

"Come on," Rhino said. "You don't have to say much. Just tell us what you know."

The talk today was about sauropods. Rhino knew a lot about them.

Sauropods were some of the largest dinosaurs ever discovered.

"You know *SAW-ro-pods*, those dinosaurs with a long neck, a tiny head, a big body, and a long tail?" Bella said.

Bella smiled at Rhino from the far end of the table. She had a lot to say.

"Their necks were incredibly long," Rhino said. "Like thirty feet for the biggest ones!"

"Can you imagine being a hundred feet from the tip of your tail to your nose?" said Bella. "Would you even know that you had a tip of the tail?"

"They couldn't hide very well," said a girl with black braids. "I mean, they couldn't even fit in most caves."

Rhino knew that the sauropods didn't have to hide. They were so big that few other dinosaurs would attack them. They grazed on plants and were fairly harmless for such huge creatures.

Rhino loved to draw pictures of sauropods. Sometimes he drew T. rex and other big meat eaters attacking the sauropods. But usually he drew them just eating from the treetops. He knew that the biggest ones had to eat hundreds of pounds of plants every day.

Rhino hoped that Cooper would say some of those things. But Cooper ate quietly while the others talked.

When lunchtime ended, Rhino tossed his sandwich wrapper in the trash can. Bella was also throwing out her garbage. Then they joined the crowd of kids trying to exit the crowded lunchroom.

"My dad thinks we'll have a very good team," Bella said.

"I hope so," Rhino said. He was also hoping that Dylan wouldn't spoil the fun for everyone.

"Dad said you're good at fielding the ball," Bella said.

"He did?" Rhino was glad to hear that Coach Ray had noticed. *Major League Baseball, here I come,* he thought.

"Yes. He said you look as if you've been practicing."

"I have," Rhino said. "My grandpa pitches to me every day after school. We play catch, too."

"My dad's been teaching me some things," Bella said. "He says the toughest part of having a new team is that a lot of kids have never played baseball at all. But we have a few who already know the basics."

Rhino nodded. He knew that he could catch and throw well. And he could hit like a champion with Grandpa. He was concerned about the heavier wooden bat, especially after what Dylan said. But Rhino would make sure to practice, practice, and practice.

"Your dad says everyone will play, right?"

"Of course," Bella said. "We'll all get an equal shot."

"That's good."

Bella glanced at the clock. "Running late," she said. "See you at practice."

"See you then," Rhino said.

He was glad that there would be a few friendly faces at practice. He hoped that would be enough to outweigh one very nasty face.

· CHAPTER 6 ·
Doubles & Dylan Troubles

The afternoon was warm with a light breeze. Rhino hurried to the field with Cooper. He looked around but didn't see Dylan.

"Maybe he won't show up," Rhino said.

"Don't count on it," Cooper replied. "He'll be here."

Coach Ray was on the pitcher's mound, tossing a ball back and forth with Bella. She took off her orange baseball cap and waved it at Rhino and Cooper.

"Start throwing," Coach said. "Spread out."

Rhino grabbed a new baseball. The smooth covering was cool in his hand. He loved how the red stitching felt in his grip. He fired the ball to Cooper.

"Whoa," Cooper said as he caught it. "Easy, Rhino!"

Rhino laughed. He was excited. "Too hot for you?" he asked.

Cooper threw it back just as hard. Rhino had to lunge for the ball.

"Be accurate!" Coach Ray called. "No sense throwing it fast if you can't throw it straight."

Cooper blushed. He stuck his tongue out at Rhino. They threw the ball easier for the next several minutes. By then, all of the players had arrived. Dylan was in the outfield by himself, tossing a ball into the air and catching it.

"Let's work on grounders now," Coach said. "Throw the ball on the ground to your partner." He showed the proper position for fielding the ball.

Later, each player got a turn at bat. Coach sent Rhino into center field. Coach did the pitching.

Rhino fielded two balls that were hit his way. But most of the players didn't hit the ball as far as the outfield.

"We need some power!" called Bella, who was in left field. She smacked her glove with her fist. No one had hit the ball in her direction yet.

It was Cooper's turn to bat.

"Get ready," Rhino called to Bella. "He's strong."

Cooper hit the first pitch right back to Coach. Since this was a practice session, each player was able to swing ten times. On his last hit, he ran the bases.

Cooper's final hit was a line drive into the outfield. The ball landed between Bella and Rhino. They both ran after it. Bella got to it first. She fired the ball toward second base. Cooper stepped onto the base just before the ball arrived.

"Nice throw!" Coach said. "Rhino and Dylan, you're the next batters."

Rhino ran fast toward the dugout. He picked up a bat and wrapped both hands around the handle. The bat seemed a bit too heavy. He grabbed a slightly smaller one. That one felt right. He made sure no one was close, then took a practice swing. He put on a batting helmet and walked proudly toward home plate.

"Ten swings," Dylan whispered as Rhino walked past. "Bet you miss every one."

Rhino could feel his face heat up. *Ignore him,* Rhino's thinker said. *He's all noise.*

Dylan kneeled in the on-deck circle, a few feet away. Rhino focused on the coach.

The first pitch was straight down the middle of the plate. The ball was moving more slowly than Grandpa James's pitches. Rhino expected to slam it.

But his swing hit nothing but air.

"Nice cut," Coach said. "You swung just a little early."

"You missed it by a mile," Dylan muttered. "Not even close."

Rhino glared at Dylan and tightened his lips, but he didn't say anything. Dylan smirked.

Rhino nicked the next pitch. It rolled behind first base. Foul ball.

"Lucky," Dylan said. "You won't hit this next one."

Coach turned his gaze to Dylan. "Let's be supportive," he said. "This is a team. We all work together."

Dylan looked at the ground.

I'll show him, Rhino thought. *This one's going over the fence. The ball is Dylan's big mouth.*

Rhino swung hard. But he missed again.

"Just make contact, Rhino," Coach said. It was the same advice Grandpa James always gave him.

Rhino could feel the sweat under his shirt now. He was warm and ready. After two more grounders, he squeezed the bat tighter.

"Last swing," Coach said. "Run this one out."

Rhino nodded. He kept his eyes on the pitcher.

The ball came a little faster, but it was straight. Rhino timed it just right. He smacked it hard. The ball took off on a line over the second baseman's head. Rhino dropped the bat and sprinted.

As Rhino reached first base, he looked toward the outfield. The right fielder was just getting to the ball, and he was nearly to the fence. Rhino rounded the base and ran harder.

From the corner of his eye, Rhino could see the outfielder throw the ball toward second. Cooper was waiting for it, just in front of the base. Rhino would have to slide.

Rhino and the ball arrived at the same time. He heard the ball hit Cooper's glove with a *smack*. Cooper lowered his glove to tag Rhino, but Rhino slid out of reach. His foot hit the base. Coach called, "Safe!"

Rhino jumped up and smiled. He and Cooper had both hit doubles.

"Yessssss!" Rhino said.

"Good base-running," Coach said. "Get your glove, Rhino. Let's give you a chance to play the infield."

Rhino trotted back to the dugout. He picked up his glove.

Coach pointed to third base. "Try that spot," he said.

Rhino set up a few feet from the base. Then he took a couple of steps back. Dylan was up.

Dylan hit the ball hard. His first few swings sent the ball into the outfield. When Coach told him to run the last one out, Dylan turned toward Rhino. He pointed with a finger, as if to say that he'd be hitting the ball over his head.

Whack! The ball sailed past the shortstop and flew into left field. It hit the fence on the first bounce. Bella and the center fielder scrambled after it.

Rhino braced as Dylan came racing around second base. The throw would be coming to third!

Dylan was charging straight toward him at full speed.

Rhino was ready. The ball was on its way, moving fast. So was Dylan.

As Dylan slid, he grabbed Rhino's leg, knocking him off balance. Rhino stumbled. He kicked free of Dylan, but the ball bounced past them both. Rhino raced to pick it up.

Rhino grabbed the ball and looked up. Dylan was standing on third base with a big grin.

"Is he allowed to grab me like that?" Rhino called to the coach.

"Definitely not," Coach said. "Did you do that on purpose, Dylan?"

Dylan shook his head. "Nope. He just got in my way."

"Well, let's be careful," Coach said. "In a game, an umpire would call you out for interfering on purpose." He told Dylan to get his glove and play right field.

Rhino tossed the ball to the coach. He felt

a shove to his shoulder as Dylan walked past. Rhino shoved back harder.

"Stop being such a baby," Dylan whispered. "You're lucky I didn't knock you over."

"You grabbed my leg on purpose."

"Watch your mouth," Dylan said. "Or you might get grabbed again after practice. On purpose."

· CHAPTER 7 ·
Let's Celebrate

Grandpa James arrived with C.J. just before practice ended. Rhino was glad to see them.

"We'll go to Roman's to celebrate your first practice," Grandpa said. "Sound good?"

Rhino nodded. He was always ready for pizza, and Roman's had the best in town.

Grandpa stopped to talk with Coach Ray for a few minutes. C.J. asked Rhino how practice had gone.

"I hit a double," Rhino said.

"A double, huh? That's great," C.J. said. "Good team?"

"I think so," Rhino replied. It all seemed good except for one teammate.

"You don't sound very enthusiastic," C.J. said. "Was there a problem?"

Rhino shook his head. "No problems. It's all good."

Grandpa jogged over. "Your coach is a nice man," he said.

"He sure is," Rhino agreed.

They were the last ones to leave the field. Other players' parents had picked them all up. But as Grandpa James pulled out of the parking lot, Rhino saw Dylan walking by himself up the hill.

"Is he on your team?" Grandpa asked.

"Yes."

"Should we offer him a ride?"

"No way!" Rhino said sharply.

C.J. turned to look at Rhino. He grinned. "I guess not," C.J. said. "He's the problem?"

Rhino looked down and scowled. "He lives nearby," he said. "So he doesn't need a ride."

But Rhino didn't really know where Dylan lived. Actually, he didn't really know anything about Dylan. He did know that he wanted nothing to do with the bully. There was no way Rhino would invite Dylan into Grandpa James's car after how he'd acted at practice.

They took a booth by the front window and ordered two pizzas and three salads. Rhino loved the smells coming from the kitchen: pizza crust and garlic and tomato sauce. His mouth was watering. "I'm starving. I could eat an entire pizza in five minutes," he said. During practice he hadn't realized how hungry he was.

"Exciting day," Grandpa said. He picked up his water glass and held it out. "Here's to Little Rhino's first day as a real baseball player." They gently clinked their glasses together as a toast.

Soon they dug into the pizza. Rhino was on his second slice when C.J. spoke up.

"So, who is that kid?" C.J. asked.

Rhino knew which kid C.J. meant. "Dylan," Rhino mumbled. "He's a pain."

"I've seen him around," C.J. said. "He's always by himself. Doesn't he have any friends?"

Rhino wasn't sure. He assumed Dylan had a few friends somewhere, but he couldn't think of any. "He picks on everybody," Rhino said. "I don't know why anyone would want to be his friend."

"You can just ignore him," C.J. said.

"He's hard to ignore," Rhino replied. "He's always saying things at school or at practice. He made me mad when I was batting."

"You have to tune that out," Grandpa said. "Concentrate on the pitcher. There will always be people trying to distract you or intimidate you when you're batting."

"Some people are poor sports," C.J. said. "I had to deal with that, too."

"How did you do it?" Rhino asked.

"Like Grandpa said, you tune it out." C.J. smiled. "The best way to shut them up is to get a hit."

Rhino nodded. Hitting that double had helped. But Dylan had been just as mean after.

"There's one other thing to remember," C.J. said. "Sometimes you can turn an enemy into a friend. It isn't easy, but I've done it. Some kids just don't know how to start."

Rhino looked at the pizza crust in his hand. He didn't want to be friends with Dylan. Why should he even try?

"Do you know what position you'll be playing?" Grandpa asked.

"Not yet," Rhino said. "I did pretty well in center field. Then Coach had me try third base. I didn't like that very much."

"At your age you should try all of the positions," Grandpa said. "You never know which one will suit you."

"Your coach will figure out where you'll do best," C.J. said. "You've got a strong arm so he might keep you at third base."

"I hope not." It was a long throw from third base to first. Plus, he'd have to field some hot grounders. "I like the outfield," he said. He would certainly make some errors at third base. Dylan would hound him about that. "You need a strong arm out in center field, too."

"The number one rule is to have fun," Grandpa said. "Number two is to play hard and learn the game."

Number three is to ignore Dylan, Rhino thought. That would be the toughest rule of all.

C.J. slid his arm toward Rhino and brought his fist against his brother's hand. "Hang in there," he said. "Be yourself."

Who else could Rhino be? He wasn't sure what C.J. meant. But he felt a lot better, anyway.

· CHAPTER 8 ·
A Diving Catch

It was much cooler during the Mustangs' next practice session. A light rain fell on and off. They worked on fielding grounders and making accurate throws. Then Coach Ray called everyone to the dugout.

"We have a practice game scheduled for Saturday," Coach said. "It won't count in the league standings, but it will be like a real game. Six innings. Three strikes and you're out. Umpires."

Rhino felt a thrill. He'd been waiting for this.

"Do we get uniforms?" Cooper asked.

"We sure do," Coach said. "Jerseys, pants, and socks. We'll hand them out after practice."

Coach opened a box that was sitting on the dugout bench. "Here's something we can use right now," he said. He lifted some blue baseball caps from the box. Each one had a big white *M* above the brim.

"Wow," Rhino said as he placed the cap on his head. He had a wide grin.

"We'll spend the rest of practice in a real game situation," Coach said. "That will help us get ready for Saturday."

Coach Ray sent Cooper to the pitcher's mound. Dylan put on the catcher's mask and other gear and set up behind the plate. The assistant coach stood behind Dylan as the umpire.

"Let's start you in center," Coach Ray said to Rhino.

Rhino grabbed his glove and sprinted to the outfield. He jumped over second base. Sandy mud splattered onto his legs. He didn't care. He smiled at Bella, who was in right field.

I hope they hit it to me every time, Rhino thought.

The first batter did just that. Cooper's pitch came in high and hard, and the batter connected. The ball soared to the gap between right field and center. Rhino raced toward it. He followed the ball as it fell toward the ground. Could he reach it in time?

Rhino stretched. The ball was out of reach. He dove toward it. He felt the ball hit his glove as he rolled in the wet grass. Did he have it?

Yes! The ball was firmly in the webbing of the glove. Coach Ray shouted, "Great play!" Rhino's teammates cheered.

Rhino tossed the ball back to the infield. He picked up his cap, which had fallen off when he dove. Then he wiped his wet hands on his shirt and jogged back to his position.

Rhino let out a deep breath. That was a great start. He was ready for more.

The next few batters did not hit the ball out of the infield. Rhino bounced on his toes to stay ready.

Then two more batters struck out. Coach Ray turned and waved his arm. "Let's bring Rhino and Cooper in," he called. He sent two players to take their places.

Rhino was excited after that great catch he'd made. He was ready to hit a home run. He picked up a bat and waited as another boy stepped up to bat.

"Dinosaur weather," Cooper said with a smile.

Rhino laughed. He pointed to his shirt, which was wet from the diving catch. "It's swampy out there."

"Great conditions for duck-billed dinos," Cooper said. "These caps make us look like them."

Rhino nodded. The bills of the caps stuck out like the beaks of the duckbills. "They'd like that wet grass," he said.

"Watch out for T. rex," Cooper said. "They preyed on the duckbills."

Soon it was Rhino's turn to bat. He was feeling great as he strode to the batter's box. He'd forget about Dylan, who was squatting behind the plate in the face mask and chest protector.

"Lucky catch," Dylan whispered. "You'll never do that again."

Ignore him, Rhino thought. That's what C.J. had told him. *I bet he wouldn't have been able to make that catch in the outfield,* Rhino thought.

The first pitch looked too low to Rhino. He watched it go by.

"Strike," called the umpire.

Rhino dug his left foot into the dirt. He concentrated on the pitcher. He'd smack this next one over the fence.

"Easy out!" Dylan called. "He's afraid to swing."

Could Dylan be any more annoying? Rhino was not afraid to swing. He gripped the bat tighter. He took a powerful cut at the pitch, but the ball was high and outside.

"Strike two," said the umpire.

Dylan laughed. "You're choking," he whispered. "Can't take the pressure."

Shut up, you bully, Rhino thought. But he didn't say it out loud.

Rhino connected with the next pitch, but the ball rolled behind third base.

"Foul ball," called the umpire.

Rhino blew out his breath. His hands stung a little. He hadn't hit that ball solidly.

This one, he thought.

The pitcher threw a fast one.

"Swing, batter!" Dylan blurted.

Rhino hesitated. The pitch was coming straight down the middle. But Dylan's words shook him. He swung too late. The ball whizzed past.

"Strike three," said the umpire.

Rhino's eyes stung. He stared at the pitcher.

"Clear out," Dylan said. "Let's get a real batter in here."

"That's enough of that," the assistant coach said. "Take off the gear, Dylan. You're done for the day."

Rhino walked back to the dugout and sat on the bench. He barely paid attention as Cooper hit a single right up the middle.

After practice, Coach handed out the rest of the equipment. "Great job today," he said to Rhino as he gave him a blue jersey with the number 6. "You made the best catch of the day. We'll start you in center field on Saturday."

That made Rhino feel confident. He knew he could hit the ball. Striking out was part of the game. And on Saturday, Dylan wouldn't be the catcher when Rhino was batting. They were teammates, even though it didn't seem like that. Teammates weren't supposed to root against each other.

Bella, Cooper, and some others were putting on their new jerseys. Rhino carefully folded his. He wanted to put it on, but he'd wait until he was home. He didn't want it to get wet or muddy. Not yet. The jersey would be clean and new for Saturday.

And Rhino would show them all that he wasn't just a great fielder. He'd hit the ball every time.

Just connect, he thought. *I'll show them that I am an awesome hitter.*

· CHAPTER 9 ·
PB&J Every Day

Rhino and Cooper wore their new baseball caps to school the next day. They weren't allowed to wear them during class. Rhino kept his in his desk. He peeked at it every few minutes. Between classes, he ran his fingers over the big white *M*.

"Mustangs!" Rhino whispered to Cooper.

Cooper gave him a thumbs-up and said the same thing.

"What did you bring for lunch?" Cooper said as they headed toward the cafeteria.

"Same as always," Rhino said. "Peanut butter and jelly. BBQ chips. An apple."

"Don't you get bored with the same lunch every day?"

Rhino laughed. "I could eat it three times a day. Every day. Except pizza day."

Rhino headed straight for the dinosaur table. Cooper stayed back, but Rhino waved him over. "Just be yourself," Rhino said, recalling what C.J. had said about him. "You know plenty about dinosaurs to speak up."

Cooper frowned. But he followed Rhino to the dinosaur table.

Today the talk was about T. rex again. No one ever got tired of talking about the giant meat-eaters. T. rex was the most feared dinosaur.

Rhino listened, but he didn't say anything yet. He took small bites of his sandwich. He wanted to make it last. He was very hungry today. He wished he had two.

"I wouldn't be scared of a T. rex," said the boy with red hair.

"*Sure* you wouldn't," Bella said. "You'd run faster than a deer if you saw one."

"I don't think they were so tough," the red-haired boy said. "I heard they might have been scavengers. They just ate animals that were already dead. Like vultures do now."

Rhino had heard that idea. But he was quite sure T. rex was a predator. They hunted other dinosaurs.

"They couldn't kill a sauropod," the boy said. "Those things were way too big."

"There were plenty of smaller dinosaurs," Bella said. "A beast like T. rex had lots of animals to prey on."

"Like what?" the boy asked. He was ready to argue.

Rhino looked across the table. "I'll bet Cooper knows."

Cooper winced, but Rhino knew he had the answer. Everyone was looking at Cooper.

Cooper swallowed hard. He took a sip of milk and kept looking down. But then he spoke. "There were lots of duckbills when T. rex lived," Cooper said. "They were gentle plant-eaters, and they were a lot smaller than the giant sauropods."

"So what?" said the redhead.

"They would have made nice meals for a T. rex," Cooper said. He finally looked up. He had a small smile on his lips. "A tasty snack." Cooper took the last bite of his sandwich and smacked his lips. Rhino and Bella laughed.

"Look who finally found his voice," said the girl with black braids. She pointed at Cooper and smiled. "Nice to see that you're awake."

Cooper blushed. The others kidded him a bit, too.

"I thought you were under special orders to stay quiet," the red-haired boy said. "Welcome to the world of talkers."

Rhino reached over and smacked hands with Cooper. He was happy for his friend and could tell that all the teasing was good-natured.

"So why did some dinosaurs have bills, anyway?" Bella asked. "Seems like a strange thing to have on your face."

Rhino knew that answer. "They ate very tough plants," he said. "The bills were like hard beaks, for chewing."

Bella picked up a hunk of bread from her plate. "I could use one of those today," she said. "This roll is stale enough to break a tooth."

The lunch period ended. "Next time let's talk about triceratops," said the girl with the braids.

Rhino didn't know much about triceratops. He'd be sure to study his dinosaur book. He needed to learn as many facts as he could. He and Cooper would both have plenty to say next time.

· CHAPTER 10 ·
Game Time

Rhino woke up early on Saturday. He hurried downstairs and ate a big bowl of cereal and an orange. Then he carefully unfolded his new jersey and held it up. The big 6 and the word MUSTANGS made him proud. He put on his uniform pants and socks, the jersey, and the cap. He liked how he looked in the mirror.

Grandpa laughed when he saw Rhino all suited up. "The game doesn't start for three hours," he said.

"I wish I could make it get here sooner," Rhino said. "Can we practice?"

"Sure," Grandpa replied. He set down his coffee cup. "But put on a different shirt for now. It's still a little wet out there."

The sun was out and there was little chance of rain, but the grass was damp. Rhino ran onto the lawn. He did twenty jumping jacks.

"Let's not overdo it." Grandpa smiled as he tossed the ball. "Save your energy for the game. We'll just warm up a little."

Rhino had never been more excited about anything. His first game. Even though it was just a practice game, it was a big deal. He could picture himself walking into a Major League stadium.

They threw the ball back and forth for a while. Rhino knew that two other teams would be having a practice game before the Mustangs played. "Can we go early to watch?" he asked.

"Yes, but it's too soon yet," Grandpa said. "Why don't you read for a half hour?"

Rhino read about triceratops. He read about Mars and Venus. He even read about football. But his mind kept turning to the baseball game. Would he make another great catch? Would he strike out? Would Dylan be a bigger pain than ever?

It seemed to take forever, but finally they drove to the field. Teams in yellow shirts and purple shirts were finishing their game. Rhino saw some of his teammates gathered in the bleachers.

When their time came, the Mustangs followed Coach Ray onto the field. It felt very different than a practice session. The bleachers were full of parents, and three umpires in blue-and-gray uniforms were waiting. The base paths had been raked and home plate was shiny clean. The grass had been cut and it smelled fresh.

Most important of all, another team was on the field. The Tigers had orange jerseys and black caps. Rhino recognized a few of the players from school. They were good athletes. Strong and fast.

Rhino and Cooper began tossing a ball back and forth. Their teammates broke into pairs and did the same.

As usual, Dylan arrived late, climbing over the fence in right field instead of entering through the gate. He ran over and picked up a ball. He threw it into the air and caught it.

Cooper's next throw was high, and Rhino had to jump to grab it. He glanced over at Dylan, who was still having a catch by himself. Rhino gripped the ball tight. Then he threw it back to Cooper.

Rhino kept looking at Dylan. No one had asked him to join their pair.

"Hey, Dylan," Rhino said. He didn't say it in a friendly way. He just wanted to get Dylan's attention.

Dylan looked over and scowled. "What?" he said.

Rhino threw him the ball. "Catch."

Dylan looked surprised. He caught the ball and threw it back to Rhino. Rhino threw it to Cooper. And Cooper threw it to Dylan.

They didn't say anything more. Rhino, Cooper, and Dylan continued their three-way catch until Coach called everyone to the dugout.

"Why'd you do that?" Cooper asked as he caught up to Rhino.

Rhino shrugged. "He needed to warm up, too." Rhino didn't like to admit it, but Dylan was a part of their team. They were all on the same side today.

"He was okay when we let him in," Rhino said. "He wasn't paired up with anybody. I think he just doesn't know how to make friends."

· CHAPTER 11 ·
Fast Pitches Mean Strikeouts

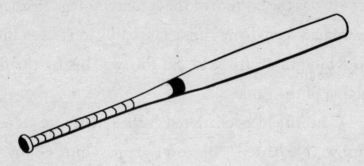

Batter up!"

Rhino's eyes grew wide. He swallowed hard. The home-plate umpire was looking at him. So was everyone else at the ballpark.

On the pitcher's mound, a tall boy was smacking his glove with his fist. He'd struck out every batter he'd faced so far. None of Rhino's teammates had even hit a foul ball.

Rhino stepped up to the plate. The pitcher sneered. He glared at Rhino. Rhino glared back. *This is the real deal. This is what Grandpa and I have been practicing for. This is what wearing my number 6 jersey is all about!*

It was the bottom of the second inning. Neither team had scored any runs. The ball hadn't been hit to Rhino in center field. So this was his first true action of the game.

The infielders chattered as the pitcher got set to throw. "No batter!" "Blaze it right past him, Gibby." "He can't hit!"

Rhino's teammates were yelling, too. "Wait for your pitch." "Blast one!"

The first pitch was faster than any Rhino had seen at practice or from Grandpa. It whizzed by before Rhino had a chance to react.

"Stee-rike!" said the umpire.

"Easy out!" came a cry from the infield.

Rhino blinked. He took a step back, then spread his feet a little wider.

He's fast, Rhino thought. *But I'm ready now.*

The next pitch was just as quick, but it looked way outside to Rhino. He let it go by.

"Ball one."

"Good eye!" yelled Cooper.

"A walk's as good as a hit," called Bella.

The pitcher kept glaring. This time, Rhino held his gaze.

Straight down the middle, Rhino thought. *Then good-bye, Mr. Baseball!*

The pitch was straight, even faster than before. Rhino timed his swing.

Pop! The bat met the ball and sent it almost straight up. The catcher stood and circled back, trying to get under it. But the ball flew over the backstop and out of play.

"Nice contact!" called Coach Ray. "Straighten it out, Rhino."

Rhino felt good now. The nerves were gone. He'd smack this next pitch into the outfield. Or farther.

But the pitch was very low. Rhino had to step back to avoid being hit in the foot.

"Ball two," said the umpire.

The chatter kept up from the field and the dugout. Rhino wiped one hand on his jersey. He gripped the bat tight.

He swung with all his might.

"Strike three!"

Rhino trudged to the bench.

"Good at bat," Coach Ray said as Rhino entered the dugout. "No one's got a hit off him yet, but he'll tire."

"Great swings," Cooper said.

"Nice job," Bella added. "You didn't go fishing at any bad pitches."

"Good eye," said another teammate.

"You stunk," said Dylan.

"Shut up," Rhino said. "You didn't do any better."

Dylan had struck out in the first inning.

Rhino frowned and wished he'd let it slide. He didn't like to lower himself to Dylan's annoying level of taunting.

The Tigers scored a run in the third, but Cooper was doing a good job pitching. He allowed only a couple of singles and walked just one batter. The game stayed tight. Rhino came up to bat again to lead off the fourth inning. The Mustangs trailed, 1–0.

Rhino was ready for the pitcher's speed now. He fouled off the first pitch, hitting it with power past the bleachers near first base.

The second pitch blazed past him, but the umpire called it a ball.

Rhino made contact with the third pitch. The foul ball banged off the fence in front of the Mustangs' dugout.

"Nice power!" Cooper called.

I've got him now, Rhino thought. He'd seen enough pitches to know the speed. He'd swing at the right moment this time.

Here came the pitch. Something was different. Rhino swung the bat and hit nothing but air. The ball plopped into the catcher's mitt. Rhino had struck out again. He blew out his breath in an angry huff.

"He got you with a changeup," Coach said as Rhino put his bat in the rack. "An off-speed pitch. Tricky."

Rhino had never expected a slow pitch at that point. *He won't fool me like that again,* his thinker said. *Next time up:* Bam!

"That kid's good," Coach said. "We won't see a better pitcher all season."

"Tough break," said Bella.

"Good effort," said Cooper.

"What a wimp," said Dylan.

Dylan never learns, Rhino thought. He looked away and kept his mouth shut this time.

Cooper and Dylan switched places in the fifth inning. Dylan pitched well. But the Tigers added a run in the top of the sixth. With two outs, they had runners on second and third. Another hit might seal the game.

"Come on, Dylan!" called some of the Mustangs. "Get this last guy out!"

Rhino didn't say anything. He rubbed his fist into his glove, ready to pounce on any ball that was hit his way.

Dylan pitched. A sharp *crack* rang out over the field.

Rhino took off. The ball was high and deep, angling toward the fence in deep right-center. Sprinting hard, Rhino kept his gaze on the ball while staying aware of the fence.

It looked like a home run for sure. It would take all his might, but Rhino jumped.

Rhino hit the fence at the same moment the ball reached his glove. He squeezed the ball, yanked it back, and rolled to the grass. Then he held his glove high so the umpires could see that he'd made the catch.

The crowd roared. The base runners stood still, their mouths hanging open.

"Incredible!" Bella shouted from right field.

"The catch of the year!" She ran over and smacked her glove against Rhino's.

The inning was over.

The score was still 2–0. The Mustangs had one last turn at bat.

Rhino couldn't stop grinning as he and Bella ran to the dugout. He rolled the ball to the pitcher's mound.

But that catch wouldn't mean much if the Mustangs lost the game. "Let's get some runs!" Rhino shouted.

· CHAPTER 12 ·
A Mustang's Mighty Hit

We need base runners," Coach Ray said as the players entered the dugout. The Mustangs had only had three runners reach base the entire game. Two walks and one weak single.

"Who's up?" Rhino asked.

"I am," said Cooper. "Then Bella and Dylan."

Rhino would bat fourth. But if the three players ahead of him all made outs, the game would be over. Rhino would be stuck with two strikeouts. Even though he'd made a terrific catch, he knew that wouldn't be enough for him. *Let me have another turn at bat,* he thought. *I'll blast it this time.*

Cooper had the team's only hit in the entire game. No one else had come close.

But Cooper struck out on just three pitches.

"He's still as fast as ever," Cooper said, nodding toward the pitcher. "He's throwing just as hard as he was in the first inning."

Rhino took the bat from Cooper. He edged out of the dugout, a few feet from the on-deck circle. Dylan was in the circle, lightly swinging a bat.

Rhino noticed Dylan looking at him. Dylan cleared his throat. "Nice catch out there," he mumbled, looking away.

"Thanks," Rhino said.

Dylan dug his toe into the dirt. He glanced past Rhino, then back. "We need some runs."

The Mustangs cheered as Bella drew a walk. She trotted to first base.

Dylan walked to the plate.

"Let's go, Dylan!" came a shout from the dugout.

The Mustangs were all standing. They shook

the fence in front of the dugout. "We want a hit!" they yelled.

Dylan delivered. He smacked the first pitch deep into left field. Bella reached second and kept running. She slid safely into third base as the ball was thrown to second. Dylan arrived before the ball. He was safe, too.

And Rhino was up to bat.

Both Bella and Dylan would score on a well-placed hit. *A single ties the game, and a home run would win it,* Rhino thought.

But Rhino hadn't hit a fair ball all game.

He squeezed the bat, keeping his eyes on the pitcher. This was pressure. The game was on the line.

The first pitch was fast. Rhino took a powerful swing. He missed.

"Strike one!"

Rhino stepped out of the batter's box. He set the bat between his knees and wiped both hands on his shirt. He took a deep breath and shook his head. Were this guy's pitches even *faster* than before?

"Three seconds!" came a call from the bleachers. It was Grandpa.

Rhino blinked. He stepped back into the box. He didn't need three seconds this time. He knew exactly what Grandpa meant. It made him relax. It got him ready.

He swung even harder at the next pitch. The ball whistled past.

"Strike two!"

"Just make contact!" Coach Ray called.

Right, Rhino thought. *Just hit it. A nice, clean single is all you need.*

The third pitch was way outside. The Tigers' catcher had to lunge to grab it. He called time-out and trotted to the mound.

The Tigers' coach walked to the mound, too. After a short talk, he went back to the dugout. The pitcher stayed in the game.

Just connect, Rhino thought.

The next pitch was fast and straight down the middle. Rhino had seen pitches like that all game. He knew when to swing. Straight and true.

Crrrack!

The ball took off on a high line drive, farther than Rhino had ever hit one. He ran at top speed toward first base, then glanced up to see a beautiful sight. The outfielders weren't even chasing the ball. It was sailing over the fence. *Going, going, gone! I'm a real hitter!* Rhino's thinker said.

A home run!

The Mustang players were leaping up and down, shouting and laughing and clapping. Bella scored first, then Dylan. They all waited by home plate as Rhino came racing around third base.

It felt almost like a dream to Rhino. He slowed a little in the final steps, then pumped his arms in the air and crossed the plate. Cooper pounded him on the back and Bella slapped his shoulder. Everyone else stuck up their hands for high fives.

All of the people in the bleachers were standing and cheering.

The Mustangs had won.

Rhino had never been happier. He looked over at the other dugout. The Tigers' pitcher had his cap pulled down toward his eyes as he stepped over the third-base line. The rest of the team looked stunned.

"Let's go shake hands," Coach Ray said. "That was a terrific effort by both teams."

Rhino led his teammates to the other dugout. The Tigers lined up with their hands out. Rhino lightly tapped each one. When he got to the pitcher, he said, "Great work."

The pitcher shook his head and gave a half smile. "That was some shot," he said. Then he pointed at Rhino. "Wait until next time." His smile became a full one.

"We'll see about that," Rhino said. He knew the pitcher was good. That made the home run even more satisfying.

Rhino felt a tap on his shoulder. He turned to see Dylan.

"Nice home run," Dylan said.

"Nice double."

"Yeah. See you next time."

Dylan walked away. He hadn't sounded friendly, but he hadn't sounded mean, either. Maybe they wouldn't be friends, but at least they could act like teammates. They could be supportive on the field.

"Great finish," Coach Ray said. "The real games start next weekend. We have two practice sessions left to get ready."

"We *are* ready!" said Rhino.

Coach laughed. "We've got a long way to go. But I like what I've seen. This season will be a lot of fun."

Rhino grabbed his glove from the dugout. He got a big hug from Grandpa and a high five from C.J.

One week until the first real game. Rhino couldn't wait.

"Hey, Grandpa," he said as they left the ball-park. "As soon as we get home, can we play some baseball in the yard?"

YOU CAN'T HIT WITHOUT A BAT!

HERE'S A SNEAK PEEK AT BOOK #2!

*B*ring it on, Little Rhino thought.

Baseball season was here! Rhino and his teammates had been practicing for two weeks. Finally, Saturday's game would be for real.

Rhino hit a game-winning home run in the Mustangs' practice game a few days earlier. He'd also made a great catch in center field. He felt confident. He was ready. Today's practice session was the last one before the opener.

"I'm going to smack another homer," Rhino said. "My new bat is awesome."

The bat was a gift from Grandpa James. He had surprised Rhino with it that morning. "You earned this," Grandpa said. Rhino had received excellent grades on his latest progress report. He worked just as hard in the classroom as he did on the baseball field. Rhino was so happy. The bat felt perfect when he swung it—almost like it was part of his body. It was the right weight and length for him, and it cut smoothly through the air.

The day was warm and sunny. Rhino pulled off his sweatshirt. He untucked his baggy white T-shirt out from his shorts. The team didn't practice in their uniforms. Then Rhino wrapped his hoodie around the new bat he had with him and set it on the dugout bench. He and his best friend Cooper were the first players to arrive at the field, as usual.

"Let's catch, Rhino," Cooper said. "We need to warm up." "Rhino" was the nickname that everyone called him, even though his real name was Ryan.

They tossed a ball back and forth. Coach Ray and his daughter, Bella, arrived a minute later. Other players started to trickle in, too. They were all wearing their bright blue caps with the big *M* for Mustangs.

Bella trotted over and winked at Rhino. "Hey, Cooper," she said, flipping her brown ponytail. "Mind if we switch? I need to work with my outfield partner." Bella had played right field in the practice game.

"Sure," Cooper replied. He looked around for someone else to throw with.

Bella punched her glove and said, "Fire it here, Rhino." She had her cap on backward.

After everyone had warmed up, Coach started a drill. "We need to develop quick hands," he said. He had one player in each group send a fast ground ball to the other.

"Field it cleanly, then release it fast," Coach said. "A quick throw can make the difference between an out and a base runner."

They worked on that for several minutes, then Coach sent the starters out to their positions. It was time for batting practice. "Play it like a real game," Coach said. "Run out every hit. You'll all get plenty of chances to swing the bat today."

Rhino sprinted to center field. He was so excited that he hopped up and down, waiting to make his first catch of the day.

He didn't wait long. The first batter looped a soft fly ball over the head of the second baseman. It looked like it would drop for a single, but Rhino darted after it.

The ball hung in the air just long enough for Rhino to get under it. He reached out his glove on the run and made the catch, then tossed the ball back to the pitcher.

"Incredible speed," said Bella, who had run over to back him up. "No one's going to get a hit if you're out here!"

Rhino blushed. *What's up with Bella lately being all nicey nice?* He trotted back to his position.

He caught another fly ball and fielded two grounders that got through for singles. Then Coach waved the three outfielders in to bat.

Rhino put on a helmet and grabbed his new bat. He stood with Bella while their teammate named Carlos took his turn at the plate. Carlos was the smallest player on the team but he was a good fielder.

"Nice bat," Bella said to Rhino. "Brand-new?"

Rhino nodded. "It's the best bat," he said. He handed it to Bella for a look.

"Too heavy," Bella said.

"It's just right for me," Rhino replied.

Rhino studied the pitcher. Dylan was a wise guy and often a bully, but he was a good athlete. He'd given Rhino a hard time early in the season, but lately he minded his own business.

I still don't trust him but he is *my teammate.* Rhino's thinker said. Grandpa had taught Rhino to always use his head and think things through.

Dylan took off his cap and ran his hand through his stiff, blond hair. He smirked at the batter, put his cap back on, and wound up to pitch.

Carlos swung and missed. Dylan laughed. His next pitch was a strike, too. Carlos finally hit a weak ground ball that Dylan fielded. His throw to first was a little high, and it bounced off the first baseman's glove and dropped to the ground.

"Don't be afraid of the ball!" Dylan yelled at the first baseman, Paul.

Paul stared at his glove and ran his other hand through his curly red hair. He had dropped another throw earlier, and he did not seem confident about playing first base.

Bella was up next and struck out. She frowned as she walked past Rhino on his way to the plate. "He's got good stuff today," she said. "Tough to hit." Dylan glared at Rhino. Rhino glared back.

Dylan is always so confident that he'll get the best of everyone, said Rhino's thinker. *I'll show him.*

Rhino stopped beside home plate. He took his bat and pointed to the outfield. "That's where this one is going," he said. Dylan shot him a dirty look as Rhino picked up a helmet from the backstop and walked around the base to get into his batting stance.

The first pitch was high and way inside. Rhino leaned back and let it go by.

The second pitch was low and outside. Rhino shook his head. "Put it in here!" he said.

"Right past you," Dylan said. He wound up and fired the ball.